Alice's Alphabet Book

Alice's Alphabet Book

A Wonderland A to Z

OXGARTH PRESS

Once upon a rhyme, a young girl called Alice went on an adventure.

She met many
creatures along the way,
so let's introduce some
without delay.

A rabbit draws Alice into Wonderland, a place full of things she cannot understand. During her travels she meets these twins, and others with such delightful grins.

White Rabbit

Tweedledum and Tweedledee

Cheshire Cat

Amongst the crowd are made-up creatures, who have the most unlikely features. In Looking Glass country she meets the hairy, and others who are ferociously SCARY.

One is a bit too portly and fat, while another wears a plain square hat. The Duchess's hat is so much finer, but doesn't impress the sneezing minor.

Carpenter

Old Father William

Duchess and Baby

Here is the star of a nursery rhyme, the other has sadly run out of time. Some are friendly and some are mad, and some are really just plain bad.

Humpty Dumpty

Dodo

Mad Hatter

Queen of Hearts

Now we
have
come
to the
end of
this trail,
we find
we have
reached
the Dor-
mouse's
tail!

With the introductions
done, so our rhyme
is now begun.

A

*is for Alice,
the star of our
rhyme*

B

is for Baby,

sneezing

all the

time

*Speak roughly to your little boy,
 And beat him when he sneezes:
He only does it to annoy,
 Because he knows it teases.*

C

*is for
Cheshire Cat,*

grinning ear to ear

D *is for the Dodo, who's no longer here*

*Everybody has won,
and all must have prizes.*

E

is for Eel, carefully balanced on your nose

F *is for*
Flamingo mallets –

G
is for Gryphon, a lion and eagle united

H *is for Humpty Dumpty, and a rhyme much recited*

Humpty Dumpty sat on a wall,
Humpty Dumpty had a great fall.
All the king's horses and all the king's men,
Couldn't put Humpty together again.

I said it very loud and clear:
I went and shouted in his ear.

I *is for the Insects, like the Rocking-horse-fly*

J

*is for Jabberwock,
who by the sword
did die*

*And, as in uffish thought he stood,
 The Jabberwock, with eyes of flame,
Came whiffling through the tulgey wood,
 And burbled as it came!*

K

is for the White Knight, falling off his horse

L is for Looking-glass

– *back-to-front of course!*

(*of course!*)

Twinkle, twinkle, little bat!
How I wonder what you're at!
Up above the world you fly
Like a tea-tray in the sky.

M

*is for
Mad Hatter,
anxious
and nervy*

N is for Nonsense,
and things
topsy-turvy

'O Oysters,' said the Carpenter,
 'You've had a pleasant run!
Shall we be trotting home again?'
 But answer came there none—
And this was scarcely odd, because
 They'd eaten every one.

O *is for Oysters, lured from their watery bed*

P

*is for the
Playing Cards,
painting
roses
red*

Q

*is for
the Queen,
commanding
others' fate*

R is for White Rabbit, who fears being late

*is for
the Sheep,
wearing glasses
to see*

T
is for
Twins, Tweedledum

*Tweedledum and Tweedledee
Agreed to have a battle;
For Tweedledum said Tweedledee
Had spoiled his nice new rattle.*

and Tweedledee

U *is for
Unicorn, fighting
for the crown*

V

*is for
Verdict,
which a
jury hands
down*

*The Queen of Hearts, she made some tarts,
  All on a summer day:
The Knave of Hearts, he stole those tarts,
  And took them quite away!*

W

is for Walrus, talking of many things

X

*is in
EXecutioner,
serving
queens
and
kings*

Y

is for a Young Deer, fond of Alice it seems

and **Z** *brings us to the end of Alice's dreams* z^{z^z}

This book reuses the original
illustrations from Lewis Carroll's
Alice's Adventures in Wonderland (1865) and
Through the Looking-Glass (1871) drawn by
John Tenniel and then engraved
by the Dalziel brothers.

A B C

The various typefaces used in this
book have been revived by the author.

This *big letter*

was probably cut by Peter de Walpergen
in Oxford in about 1686. This small letter
is probably of French and Dutch origin.
This *script* is based on some copper
engravings made in Oxford in the
late seventeenth century.

☞ Oxgarth Press creates
books and ephemera relating to
Oxford, the dodo, and Lewis Carroll's
Alice in Wonderland, all designed
to entertain and delight.

www.oxgarth.co.uk

*Dedicated
to my family,
with love*

Published by Oxgarth Press
1 Cleeves Avenue, Chipping Norton,
Oxfordshire, OX7 5PB
www.oxgarth.co.uk

Copyright Michael Johnson 2019
Database right Oxgarth Press (maker)
Oxgarth is a registered trademark

First edition 2019

ISBN 978 0 9534438 6 4

The moral rights of the author have been asserted. All rights reserved. No part of this publication may be reproduced, stored in a retrieval system, or transmitted, in any form or by any means, electronic, mechanical, photocopying, recording, or otherwise, without the prior permission in writing of the publisher and copyright owner. Any enquiries regarding any extracts or re-use of any material in this book should be addressed to the publisher at the address shown above. You must not circulate this book in any other binding or cover and you must impose this same condition on any acquirer.

British Library Cataloguing in Publication Data. A catalogue record for this book is available from the British Library.

Printed in the United Kingdom by
Bell & Bain Ltd, Thornliebank, Glasgow

Begin at the beginning,
the King said, very gravely,
and go on till you come to the end:
then stop